THE
TAILOR
OF
GLOSTER

MRS
TITTLE-
MOUSE

SQUIRREL NUTKIN

NUTS

TOM KITTEN

RABBIT

A STORY FOR NORAH

Frederick Warne has a continuing commitment to reproduce Beatrix Potter's exquisite watercolours to the highest possible standard. In 1993 and 1994, taking advantage of the latest advances in printing technology and expertise, entirely new film was made from her original book illustrations. The drawings are now reproduced with a quality and a degree of authenticity never before attainable in print.

FREDERICK WARNE

Published by the Penguin Group
27 Wrights Lane, London W8 5TZ, England
Penguin Books USA Inc., 375 Hudson Street, New York, N.Y. 10014, USA
Penguin Books Australia Ltd, Ringwood, Victoria, Australia
Penguin Books Canada Ltd, 10 Alcorn Avenue, Toronto, Ontario, Canada M4V 3B2
Penguin Books (N.Z.) Ltd, 182-190 Wairau Road, Auckland 10, New Zealand

Penguin Books Ltd, Registered Offices: Harmondsworth, Middlesex, England

First published 1903 by Frederick Warne
This edition with new reproductions of Beatrix Potter's book illustrations first
published 1996

Colour reproduction by
Saxon Photolitho Ltd, Norwich
Printed and bound in Great Britain by
William Clowes Limited, Beccles and London

THE TALE OF
SQUIRREL NUTKIN

❋

BY BEATRIX POTTER

F.WARNE & CO

THIS is a Tale about a tail—a tail that belonged to a little red squirrel, and his name was Nutkin.

He had a brother called Twinkleberry, and a great many cousins: they lived in a wood at the edge of a lake.

IN the middle of the lake there is an island covered with trees and nut bushes; and amongst those trees stands a hollow oak-tree, which is the house of an owl who is called Old Brown.

ONE autumn when the nuts were ripe, and the leaves on the hazel bushes were golden and green—Nutkin and Twinkleberry and all the other little squirrels came out of the wood, and down to the edge of the lake.

THEY made little rafts out of twigs, and they paddled away over the water to Owl Island to gather nuts.

Each squirrel had a little sack and a large oar, and spread out his tail for a sail.

THEY also took with them an offering of three fat mice as a present for Old Brown, and put them down upon his door-step.

Then Twinkleberry and the other little squirrels each made a low bow, and said politely—

"Old Mr. Brown, will you favour us with permission to gather nuts upon your island?"

BUT Nutkin was excessively impertinent in his manners. He bobbed up and down like a little red *cherry*, singing—

"Riddle me, riddle me, rot-tot-tote!
A little wee man, in a red red coat!
A staff in his hand, and a stone in his throat;
If you'll tell me this riddle, I'll give you a groat."

Now this riddle is as old as the hills; Mr. Brown paid no attention whatever to Nutkin.

He shut his eyes obstinately and went to sleep.

THE squirrels filled their little sacks with
nuts, and sailed away home in the evening.

But next morning they all came back again
to Owl Island; and Twinkleberry and the
others brought a fine fat mole, and laid it on
the stone in front of Old Brown's doorway,
and said—
"Mr. Brown,
will you
favour us with
your gracious
permission to
gather some
more nuts?"

BUT Nutkin, who had no respect, began to dance up and down, tickling old Mr. Brown with a *nettle* and singing—

> "Old Mr. B! Riddle-me-ree!
> Hitty Pitty within the wall,
> Hitty Pitty without the wall;
> If you touch Hitty Pitty,
> Hitty Pitty will bite you!"

Mr. Brown woke up suddenly and carried the mole into his house.

HE shut the door in Nutkin's face. Presently
a little thread of blue *smoke* from a wood fire
came up from the top of the tree, and Nutkin
peeped through the key-hole and sang—

     "A house full, a hole full!
     And you cannot gather a bowl-full!"

THE squirrels searched for nuts all over the
island and filled their little sacks.

But Nutkin gathered oak-apples—yellow
and scarlet—and sat upon a beech-stump
playing marbles, and watching the door of
old Mr. Brown.

ON the third day the squirrels got up very early and went fishing; they caught seven fat minnows as a present for Old Brown.

They paddled over the lake and landed under a crooked chestnut tree on Owl Island.

TWINKLEBERRY and six other little squirrels each carried a fat minnow; but Nutkin, who had no nice manners, brought no present at all. He ran in front, singing—

"The man in the wilderness said to me,
'How many strawberries grow in the sea?'
I answered him as I thought good—
'As many red herrings as grow in the wood.'"

But old Mr. Brown took no interest in riddles—not even when the answer was provided for him.

ON the fourth day the squirrels brought a present of six fat beetles, which were as good as plums in *plum-pudding* for Old Brown. Each beetle was wrapped up carefully in a dock-leaf, fastened with a pine-needle pin.

But Nutkin sang as rudely as ever—

"Old Mr. B! riddle-me-ree
Flour of England, fruit of Spain,
Met together in a shower of rain;
Put in a bag tied round with a string,
If you'll tell me this riddle, I'll give you a ring!"

Which was ridiculous of Nutkin, because he had not got any ring to give to Old Brown.

THE other squirrels hunted up and down the nut bushes; but Nutkin gathered robin's pincushions off a briar bush, and stuck them full of pine-needle pins.

ON the fifth day the squirrels brought a present of wild honey; it was so sweet and sticky that they licked their fingers as they put it down upon the stone. They had stolen it out of a bumble *bees'* nest on the tippitty top of the hill.

But Nutkin skipped up and down, singing—

"Hum-a-bum! buzz! buzz! Hum-a-bum buzz!
As I went over Tipple-tine
I met a flock of bonny swine;
Some yellow-nacked, some yellow backed!
They were the very bonniest swine
That e'er went over Tipple-tine."

OLD Mr. Brown turned up his eyes in disgust at the impertinence of Nutkin.

But he ate up the honey!

The squirrels filled their little sacks with nuts.

But Nutkin sat upon a big flat rock, and played ninepins with a crab apple and green fir-cones.

ON the sixth day, which was Saturday, the
squirrels came again for the last time; they
brought a new-laid *egg* in a little rush basket
as a last parting present for Old Brown.

But Nutkin ran in front laughing, and
shouting—

"Humpty Dumpty lies in the beck,
With a white counterpane round his neck,
Forty doctors and forty wrights,
Cannot put Humpty Dumpty to rights!"

NOW old Mr. Brown took an interest in eggs; he opened one eye and shut it again. But still he did not speak.

NUTKIN became more and more impertinent—

"Old Mr. B! Old Mr. B!
Hickamore, Hackamore, on the King's
    kitchen door;
All the King's horses, and all the
    King's men,
Couldn't drive Hickamore, Hackamore,
Off the King's kitchen door."

Nutkin danced up and down like a *sunbeam*;
but still Old Brown said nothing at all.

NUTKIN began again—

"Arthur O'Bower has broken his band,
He comes roaring up the land!
The King of Scots with all his power,
Cannot turn Arthur of the Bower!"

Nutkin made a whirring noise to sound like the *wind*, and he took a running jump right onto the head of Old Brown! . . . .

Then all at once there was a flutterment and a scufflement and a loud "Squeak!"

The other squirrels scuttered away into the bushes.

WHEN they came back very cautiously, peeping round the tree—there was Old Brown sitting on his door-step, quite still, with his eyes closed, as if nothing had happened.

     *   *   *   *   *

But Nutkin was in his waistcoat pocket!

THIS looks like the end of the story; but it isn't.

Old Brown carried Nutkin into his house, and held him up by the tail, intending to skin him; but Nutkin

pulled so very hard that his tail broke in two, and he dashed up the staircase and escaped out of the attic window.

AND to this day, if you meet Nutkin up a tree and ask him a riddle, he will throw sticks at you, and stamp his feet and scold, and shout—

    "Cuck-cuck-cuck-cur-r-r-cuck-k-k!"

THE END